STAR TR

STARFLEET LOGBOOK

by Jake Black

U.S.S. ENTERPRISE
NCC-1701

PSS!
PRICE STERN SLOAN
An Imprint of Penguin Random House

PRICE STERN SLOAN
Penguin Young Readers Group
An Imprint of Penguin Random House LLC

TM & © 2016 CBS Studios Inc. STAR TREK and related marks and logos are trademarks of CBS Studios Inc. All rights reserved. Published by Price Stern Sloan, an imprint of Penguin Random House LLC, 345 Hudson Street, New York, New York 10014. *PSS!* is a registered trademark of Penguin Random House LLC. Manufactured in China.

Photo credits: p.ii, 3, 4, 7, 8, 10–17, 27–31, 41, 45–48, 52, 57, 60, 61, 73–77, 81, 86–92, 95, 97, 98, 102, 105–109 © Thinkstock/Ingram Publishing; p.79, 85, © Thinkstock/goir

ISBN 978-0-399-53953-4   10 9 8 7 6 5 4 3 2 1

Welcome aboard the *U.S.S. Enterprise*, the finest ship in all of Starfleet. This logbook is designed to complete your training as an officer aboard this ship. There are lots of activities, which will prepare you to assume command of a starship of your own. Along the way, you'll complete personal log entries, recording your thoughts, adventures, and experiences as you rise through the ranks. The crew of the *Enterprise* will accompany you on each mission and activity to make sure you're as successful as possible.

James T. Kirk

Captain, *U.S.S. Enterprise*

Table of Contents

STARFLEET ACADEMY

Every Starfleet officer begins their service by attending and graduating from Starfleet Academy. Located on Earth, in San Francisco, Starfleet Academy is known as being the best educational institution on any planet throughout the quadrant.

Educational Background

EX ASTRIS, SCIENTIA

Cadets come to Starfleet Academy from other schools all over the galaxy. Tell us about your school by answering the questions below.

What is the name of your school?

Where is it located?

What grade are you in?

What is your favorite subject?

What activities do you like to participate in at school?

What is your teacher's name?

What do you wish was different about your school?

Starfleet Academy cadets live on campus in dorm rooms. Color the door hanger. Then cut it out using safety scissors and hang it on your bedroom doorknob to show the world that you're a hardworking Starfleet cadet.

EX ASTRIS, SCIENTIA

STARFLEET ACADEMY DORM ROOM

STARFLEET
CADET
STUDYING

DO NOT
DISTURB

Class Registration

Welcome to Starfleet Academy. Choose your favorite classes from the list below:

- ❑ Command School
- ❑ Security Officer Combat Training
- ❑ Basics of Dilithium Crystals
- ❑ Interstellar Biology
- ❑ Starship Mechanics
- ❑ Basic Medicine
- ❑ Plants of Vulcan
- ❑ Jonathan Archer's Federation History

ADVENTURE STUDY

Welcome to Mission Study class. Your assignment is to review an adventure of the crew of the *U.S.S. Enterprise*. Fill in the dialogue and draw in the missing pieces of the story to create your own comic book telling of this adventure. You can draw planets, aliens, or whatever you want to tell the story.

Kobayashi Maru

Every Starfleet cadet needs to take the *Kobayashi Maru* test (where a ship with that name is under attack by Klingons). This test is one of skill, but it is also called a "no-win scenario." Starfleet captains need to learn that sometimes there may be no way to "win" in a given situation. Only one cadet has ever beaten this training simulation—James T. Kirk. Play this game with a friend, using pennies as game pieces. Place your pennies at the Starfleet Academy starting space, and take turns moving around the game board. On your turn, flip a coin—move ahead two spaces for heads, one space for tails. The first player to rescue the *Kobayashi Maru* from the Klingon attack wins. But beware. You might get trapped in the no-win scenario, or even have your ship destroyed by the Klingons! If those things happen, start the game over and try again.

Start

Receive distress call from *Kobayashi Maru*.
JUMP AHEAD ONE SPACE.

Take a hit from a Klingon ship.
GO BACK ONE SPACE.

Beam aboard some injured officers from *Kobayashi Maru*.
JUMP AHEAD ONE SPACE.

Try desperate rescue attempt. **JUMP AHEAD THREE SPACES.**

You Win!

You made it! You beat the no-win scenario! You rescued the crew of the *Kobayashi Maru* and defeated the Klingons!

Rescue attempt fails. Locked in no-win scenario. **GO BACK THREE SPACES.**

Klingons destroy your ship. **GO BACK TO START.**

Figure out how to rig the test to your favor. **JUMP AHEAD FIVE SPACES.**

Abandon ship! **GO BACK TO START.**

STARFLEET QUIZ

Think you know about Starfleet? Take the quiz below and find out!

1. Who was the first captain of the *U.S.S. Enterprise* NCC-1701?
   A. Jonathan Archer
   B. Robert April
   C. Christopher Pike
   D. James T. Kirk

2. True or False: Spock was the first Vulcan to serve in Starfleet.

3. About how many crew members serve aboard the *Enterprise* NCC-1701?
   A. 100
   B. 236
   C. 430
   D. 1000

4. What alien race made the first contact with humans?
   A. Vulcans
   B. Klingons
   C. Romulans
   D. Tribbles

5. True or False: The *Enterprise* is armed with quantum torpedoes.

6. True or False: The Klingon and Romulan empires are members of the Federation.

7. The headquarters of the United Federation of Planets is found on what planet?
   A. Talos IV
   B. Kronos
   C. Ceti Alpha V
   D. Earth

10. What piece of equipment did Dr. McCoy leave behind on Sigma Iotia II?
    A. Tricorder
    B. Communicator
    C. Phaser
    D. Medical scanner

8. What musical instrument does Spock know how to play?
   A. Piano
   B. Vulcan lute
   C. Ukulele
   D. Andorian harmonica

9. What species is found on the planet Neural?
   A. Gorn
   B. Mugato
   C. Melkotians
   D. Elasians

Cadet's Log

What was your experience at Starfleet Academy (or your school) like? Write a journal entry of some of your best memories and experiences at school on the next few pages.

GRADUATION PARTY PLANNER

With your training at Starfleet Academy complete, you're ready to go on adventures aboard a starship! But first let's celebrate your training success with a party!

When is the party?

....

....

Where is the party?

....

....

Who will you invite?

....

....

....

What food will you eat?

....

....

What activities will be available?

....

....

What games will you play?

....

....

How should people dress for the party?

....

....

What gifts do you hope they will bring?

....

....

....

When will the party end?

....

....

Letter Home

To be successful at Starfleet Academy, or any other school, a person needs lots of support from family and friends. Write a thank-you note to someone who has helped you in school.

....

....

....

....

....

....

....

....

....

....

....

How would you like some model starships to play with or display? Color the ships on the following pages. Then, using safety scissors, cut out each ship and its base. You can pretend that you're going on an adventure!

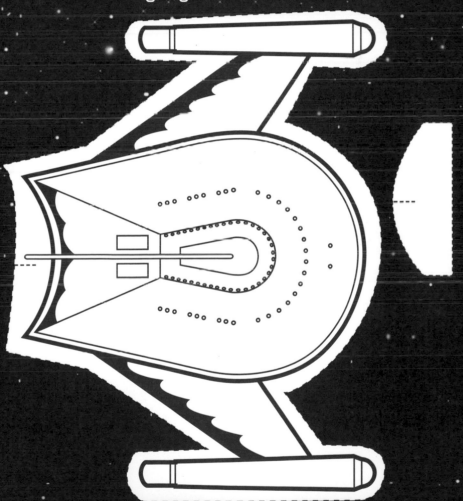

Romulan
Bird of Prey

U.S.S.
Enterprise

SHIP'S OPERATIONS

You've made it through Starfleet Academy, and now it's time for your first assignment aboard a Starfleet vessel. You've been assigned to the operations division aboard the *Enterprise*. This includes communications, security, and engineering. The division's color is red, so crew members assigned here wear red uniforms. You will be a key part of helping the *Enterprise* complete its five-year mission. Welcome aboard.

Crew Member Bios

Name: Montgomery Scott

Rank: Lieutenant Commander
Born: Aberdeen, Scotland, Earth
Current Assignment: Chief engineer
Duties: Ensure the ship runs at optimum speed and capacity
Nickname: Scotty
Famous Quote: "I'm giving it all she's got!"

Name: Nyota Uhura

Rank: Lieutenant
Born: United States of Africa, Earth
Current Assignment: Communications officer
Duties: All communications and linguistics functions aboard the *Enterprise*
Nickname: Uhura, which means "Freedom."
Famous Quote: "Hailing frequencies open."

Name: Janice Rand

Rank: Yeoman
Born: Earth
Current Assignment: Captain's yeoman
Duties: Clerical work and record keeping; roster tracking
Nickname: None
Famous Quote: "Why don't you go chase an asteroid?"

Name: John Kyle

Rank: Lieutenant
Born: British Commonwealth, Earth
Current Assignment: Transporter chief
Duties: Operate the transporter and maintain its functionality
Nickname: None
Famous Quote: "Energizing!"

SECURITY DETAIL

Captain Kirk is doing some phaser target practice. Follow each beam to match the target with each of his attempts.

Communications

Uhura has intercepted a scrambled message. Help her unscramble the message and report it to Captain Kirk by writing it out in the space provided.

*Pshi ni gadenr. Dene
Eeirsnprte to urcees su.*

CODED MESSAGES

Sometimes when you're on a mission, you need to send a coded message to other ships or to your fellow crew members. Using the key below, decode the message on the next page.

A=Z B=Y C=X D=W E=V

F=U G=T H=S I=R J=Q

K=P L=O M=N N=M O=L

P=K Q=J R=I S=H T=G U=F

V=E W=D X=C Y=B Z=A

YVZN FH FK, HXLGGB!

Now that you know how to decode messages, use these pages to write and share coded messages with your friends and have them respond with coded messages of their own.

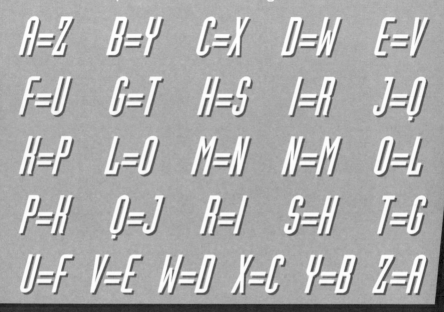

A=Z B=Y C=X D=W E=V

F=U G=T H=S I=R J=Q

K=P L=O M=N N=M O=L

P=K Q=J R=I S=H T=G

U=F V=E W=D X=C Y=B Z=A

Transporter

Chief engineer Scott is using the transporter to beam up a landing party. Help him bring the team home safely by connecting the dots for the three members of the away team.

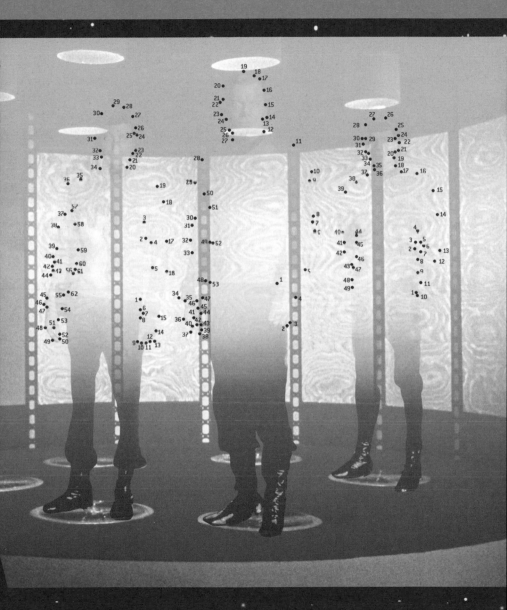

Shore Leave Journal

Starfleet officers love taking vacations, called shore leave. Sometimes crazy stuff happens on shore leave—you might meet the white rabbit from *Alice in Wonderland*, or you could dress up like a princess. What is your favorite vacation memory? What is your dream vacation to take someday? Write about it on the next few pages.

Color the *Enterprise* operations officers and Mirror Universe Kirk and Spock. Then, using safety scissors, cut out the figures and their bases. You can pretend that they're going on an adventure and helping the *Enterprise* complete their mission.

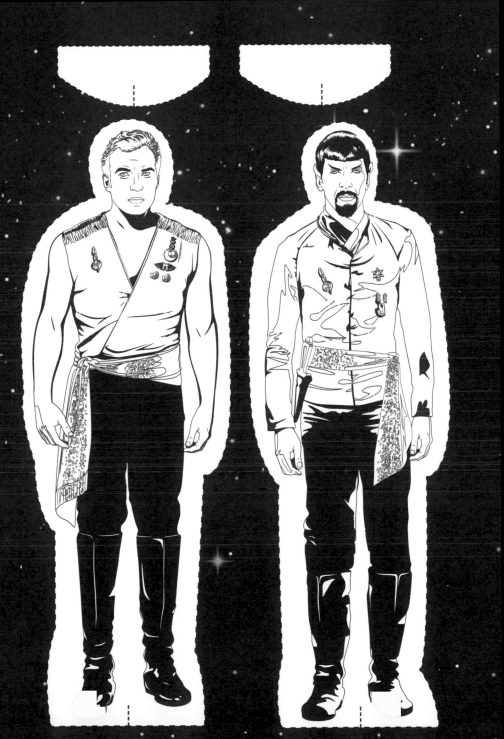

Check out the word search below. Look up, down, diagonally, forward, and backward to find the words listed below!

```
D G V V H L P X I U L A R S Y
E N T E R P R I S E R A E C O
T F A R C E L T T U H S T O C
K E Y L O V N W H U P G R T C
C C Z I P T C U N N N J O T M
K Z O A F H A W K I R K P Y U
A L D P E P J C R C V Y S F F
V M I K S H B E I C G J N Z D
Z A O N T X E S Z N U J A P N
S V D A G N K Y C S U W R T Q
J D H A I O F U B T U M T D U
Y Q B G L V N P P Z W L M T M
K X N E B M R E S A H P U O H
F E K F Z T H I R F R A I E C
G G B X K X B M J J J V V O L U
```

KIRK	SULU	COMMUNICATOR
SPOCK	CHEKOV	PHASER
MCCOY	*ENTERPRISE*	TRANSPORTER
SCOTTY	SHUTTLE CRAFT	ENGINEERING
UHURA		KLINGON

Time Travel Report

Occasionally, the crew of the *Enterprise* travels backward in time by sling-shotting the *Enterprise* around the sun at top speed, or by using a time portal like the Guardian of Forever (pictured below). Write a story about traveling back in time: What happened to you when you went into the past?

....

....

....

....

....

....

....

....

....

....

....

....

....

Engineering

Chief engineer Scott is always designing what he thinks starships will look like in the future. In the space provided below, design your own starship.

ENGINEER'S LOG

Starfleet officers record logs, which are journals of their adventures in space. Write a journal entry about your adventures today. You can talk about anything! Just write down your thoughts and feelings, and record it as your log.

....

....

....

....

....

....

....

....

....

....

SCIENCES

Your next assignment on board the *Enterprise* is to work with the sciences division. Here you will find all sorts of science, and even medicine. This division's color is blue. Truly, this is where you can "explore strange new worlds; seek out new life and new civilizations."

Crew Member Bios

Name: Spock

Rank: Commander
Born: Vulcan (half human/half Vulcan)
Current Assignment: Science officer/first officer
Duties: Study scientific elements pertaining to missions. Counsel Captain Kirk
Nickname: None
Famous Quote: "Live long and prosper."

Name: Leonard H. McCoy

Rank: Lieutenant Commander
Born: Georgia, United States, Earth
Current Assignment: Chief medical officer
Duties: Oversee the physical and mental health of the crew of the *Enterprise*
Nickname: Bones
Famous Quote: "I'm a doctor, not a bricklayer."

Name: Christine Chapel

Rank: Ensign
Born: Earth
Current Assignment: Head nurse
Duties: Assist Dr. McCoy in the care of the crew members aboard the *Enterprise*
Nickname: Nurse
Famous Quote: "There are unpleasant surprises as well as pleasant ones."

Medical

Dr. McCoy is an expert in the physiology of beings from all over the galaxy. Look at the pictures and match them with the names listed below.

SALT CREATURE   MUGATO   TELLARITE
VULCAN   TALOSIAN   TRIBBLE
ORION   GORN   KLINGON
ANDORIAN

1.

- - - - - - - - - - - - -

2.

- - - - - - - - - - - - -

3.
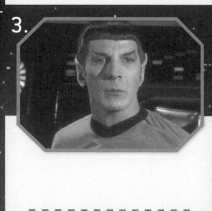

- - - - - - - - - - - - -

4.

- - - - - - - - - - - - -

TRICORDER READOUT

Tricorders are amazing devices. They can scan the air, determine someone's health, and recognize nearby life-forms. Use the tricorder above to draw a picture of the weather, and answer these questions:

How many life-forms are in the room? How do they feel physically? What is going on around you?

SCIENCE OFFICER

Mr. Spock records a log of his daily activities. You should, too. In the space provided, log any experiments, experiences, results, and questions from today. Mr. Spock doesn't write about his feelings, but you can!

_____

_____

_____

_____

_____

_____

_____

_____

_____

_____

_____

_____

FIRST CONTACT

Vulcans are an intelligent species, and they are very good at science. They were the first aliens to interact with humans. Since that first encounter, Vulcans have spent time teaching humans about their culture. You can learn about Vulcans below.

Vulcan Salute	This hand salute means "live long and prosper" or "peace and long life."
Vulcan Science Academy	In their youth, the smartest Vulcans attend school here, learning how to control their emotions while studying science and Vulcan philosophy.

IDIC

This symbol represents IDIC: Infinite Diversity in Infinite Combinations. This is the foundation of Vulcan philosophy.

Weaponry

Vulcans abhor violence, but since ancient times, they have used these unique weapons when conflicts must be settled through battle.

Identify the Alien Race

How well do you know the enemies of the Federation? Use logic and reasoning to figure out their names from the clues, and fill out the crossword puzzle.

Across

1. Klingon who hates tribbles
4. Ancient Greek god
7. Powerful teenage boy
8. Rapidly reproducing furballs
10. 1920s-style gangster leader

Down

1. Genetically superior human
2. All-powerful mischievous child
3. Lizard-like alien
5. Wild west gunslinger
6. Scoundrel who created android women
9. Legendary Klingon emperor

LANDING PARTY PLANNING

Members of the science and medical team are frequently assigned to go on planetary missions. Use the checklist for your next landing-party mission/road trip!

❑ Vehicle to travel in
❑ Rations/snacks
❑ Games to play
❑ Something to read
❑ Pillows
❑ Someone to drive

❑ Someone to navigate
❑ A planned destination
❑ Map or GPS
❑ Extra supplies
❑ Water

Science: Vulcan or Romulan

Centuries ago, the Vulcans and the Romulans were one race. But then they separated and began living on different planets. Someday they may seek reunification, but until then, they are enemies. Check out the pictures below and see if you can tell which are the Vulcans and which are the Romulans, and write your answer in the space provided.

1. _____

2. _____

3. _____

4. _____

5. _____

6. _____

7. _____

8. _____

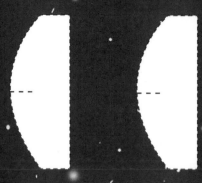

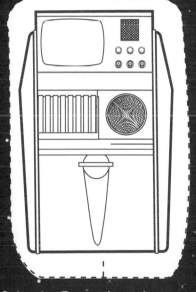

Color the *Enterprise* science and medical officers and their tricorder on the following the pages. Then, cut out the figures and their stands. You can pretend that they're going on an adventure and helping the *Enterprise* complete its mission. Beware the Klingon warrior Kor!

Fill in the blank squares below. Each row, column, and three-by-three box should contain the numbers one through nine. No row, column, or box should have the same number repeated twice.

9	1	8		3	5		6	7
3	6		8	9	4	5		2
2		5		1	7	9		3
8	7	6	9	2		3	4	5
1			4	5	3	6		8
4	5		7		8	2	9	1
	2	9	1		6			4
6			3		2			9
7		4	5		9		2	6

Ship's Historian

The crew of the *Enterprise* encountered a powerful alien named Trelane. Trelane loved the art, poetry, and music from Earth's history. As ship's historian, help Trelane learn about Earth's culture by completing the following activities:

Help Trelane understand poetry by writing a poem about your favorite thing.

....

....

....

....

....

....

....

....

....

....

....

Create a "painting" for Trelane by drawing something in the space below.

Teach Trelane the power of music by writing a song about someone or something you love.

COMMAND

You've risen through the ranks and are now a command-division officer! Dressed in gold, you are now authorized to command the ship. This includes leading as the ship's captain, or controlling the ship as helmsman or navigator. In the command division, you "boldly go where no man has gone before."

Crew Member Bios

Name: James Tiberius Kirk

Rank: Captain
Born: Iowa, United States, Earth
Current Assignment: Commanding officer
Duties: Oversee and lead all functions aboard the *Enterprise*
Nickname: Jim
Famous Quote: "Sometimes a feeling is all we humans have to go on."

Name: Hikaru Sulu

Rank: Lieutenant
Born: San Francisco, United States, Earth
Current Assignment: Helmsman
Duties: Control the flight patterns of the *Enterprise*
Nickname: None
Famous Quote: "May the Great Bird of the Galaxy bless your planet!"

Name: Pavel Andreievich Chekov

Rank: Ensign
Born: Russia, Earth
Current Assignment: Navigator
Duties: Chart flight plans for the *Enterprise*
Nickname: None
Famous Quote: "It was invented in Russia!"

MIRROR UNIVERSE

MIRROR UNIVERSE

In a parallel universe, called the Mirror Universe, the crew of the *Enterprise* is a group of barbaric tyrants who conquer planets and destroy life rather than explore the universe. They dress differently, and even have different physical appearances. (Spock has a beard!) What would your life be like in the Mirror Universe? Describe it below, and draw a self-portrait of your Mirror Universe self in the space provided.

Color the *Enterprise* command officers and the phaser on the following pages. Then, using safety scissors, cut out the figures and their stands. You can pretend that they're going on an adventure and helping the *Enterprise* complete its mission.

Maze

Ensign Chekov is a skilled navigator. That means he figures out the paths the *Enterprise* needs to take to get to its destinations. Help him navigate this maze to reach the planet.

Tholian Web

The Tholians are a dangerous species that use their ships to create a grid-like web to capture enemy ships. Play this game with a friend. Each player takes a turn connecting the dots below, one line at a time (the lines should be horizontal or vertical, not diagonal), to make a square. When you complete a square, put your initials in it. Then you get to take another turn. You can use your opponent's lines to make the squares that make up the Tholian Web. Once all the squares have been made, the player who made the most squares wins!

LESSONS FROM LINCOLN

Starship captains are leaders. They use their morals and principles to guide their ships and crews. Captain Kirk's leadership hero was Abraham Lincoln. He learned a lot from Lincoln, especially when they teamed up to fight evil together on an alien planet.

A projection of Lincoln created by an alien race taught Kirk: "We fight on their level, with trickery, brutality, finality; we match their evil." And "There is no honorable way to kill. No gentle way to destroy. There is nothing good in war, except its ending."

What lessons have you learned from leaders? Write them down in the space provided.

....

....

....

....

....

....

....

Design an Award

Starfleet awards medals and other honors for exemplary service. Design an award you'd like to receive from Starfleet, and put it on your dress uniform, like Captain Kirk and Spock do.

HIDDEN PICTURE COLOR BY NUMBER

Captain Kirk has intercepted a scrambled visual message on the view screen. Use crayons, colored pencils, or markers and the numbered color key to help unscramble it.

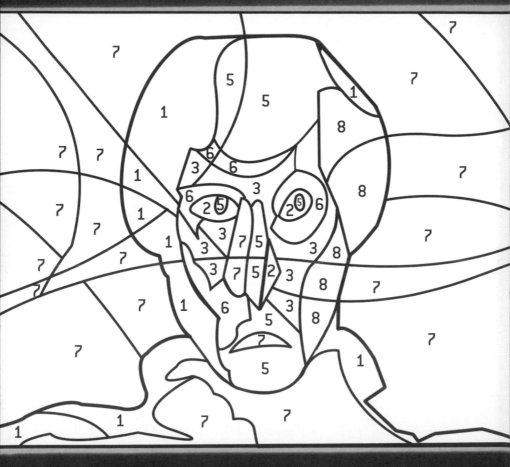

1=Red   3=Blue   5=Green   7=Black
2=Yellow   4=Orange   6=Purple   8=Pink

MEMORY CHALLENGE

How's your memory? Study this scene and then turn the page and answer the questions about it.

MEMORY QUIZ

Okay, do you think you're ready? You memorized the scene on the previous page? Answer the questions below. But remember, NO PEEKING!

1. How many crew members are in the picture?

----

2. Where does the scene take place?

----

3. How many people are sitting?

----

4. How many people are standing?

----

5. What color is Captain Kirk's uniform?

----

6. What is Sulu holding?

----

7. Are there any enemies in the scene?

CAPTAIN'S LOG

What happened today? Captain Kirk needs to record the captain's log for today's events. Record your own captain's log about stuff that happened to you today.

_____

_____

_____

_____

_____

_____

_____

_____

_____

_____

_____

_____

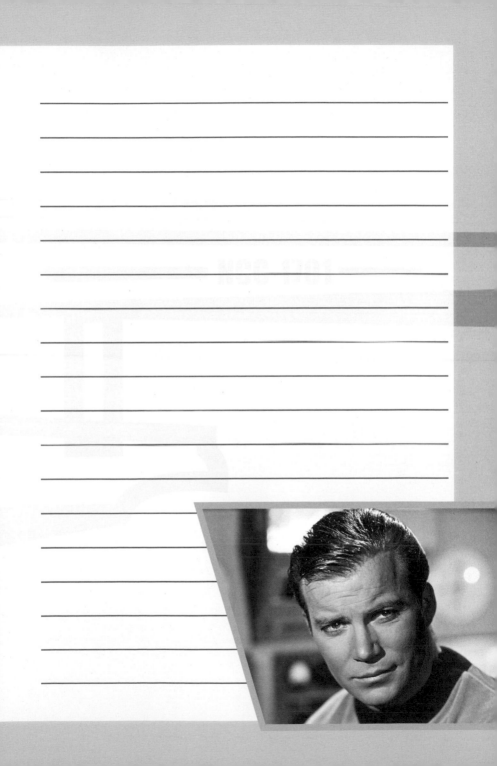

STARFLEET
ACHIEVEMENT CERTIFICATE

Congratulations. You have achieved
all there is to achieve as a Starfleet
officer. Using safety scissors, cut out
your certificate and show it off to the
world . . . this world, or whatever
strange new worlds you discover!

STARFLEET ACADEMY

presents this certificate to:

....

(your name)

In recognition of achievement in
services to Starfleet.

_____

date

ANSWERS

Starfleet Quiz (Page 18–19):

1:B; 2:F; 3:C; 4:A; 5:F; 6:F; 7:D; 8:B;
9:B; 10:B

Squiggle Maze
(Page 34):

Scrambled Message

(Page 35): Ship in danger. Need
-*Enterprise* to rescue us.

Coded Message

(Page 37): Beam us up, Scotty!

Transport Connect the Dots
(Page 41):

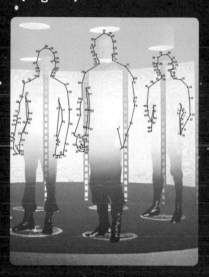

Word Search
(Page 49):

9	1	8		3	5			
3	6		8	9	4	5		
2		5		1	7	9		
8	7	6	9	2		3		
1			4	5	3	6		
4	5		7		8	2		
	2	9	1		6			
6			3		2			
7		4	5		9			

Maze (Page 91):

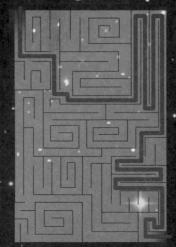

Hidden Coloring Picture

(Page 96):

Memory Quiz

(Page 97–98):

1. Four

2. *Enterprise* bridge

3. One

4. Three

5. Gold

6. A foil or sword

7. No